To Marie–Louise and Michael
M.M.

For my granddaughter Fiona
Z.C–L.

First published 2019 by Walker Books Ltd, 87 Vauxhall Walk, London SE11 5HJ • This edition published 2020 • Text © 2019 Mary Murphy • Illustrations © 2019 Zhu Cheng-Liang
The right of Mary Murphy and Zhu Cheng-Liang to be identified as author and illustrator respectively of this work has been asserted by them in accordance with the Copyright, Designs
and Patents Act 1988 • This book has been typeset in Cantarell • Printed in China • All rights reserved. No part of this book may be reproduced, transmitted or stored in an information
retrieval system in any form or by any means, graphic, electronic or mechanical, including photocopying, taping and recording, without prior written permission from the publisher
British Library Cataloguing in Publication Data: a catalogue record for this book is available from the British Library • ISBN 978-1-4063-9299-9 • www.walker.co.uk • 10 9 8 7 6 5 4 3 2 1

What I Like Most

MARY MURPHY

illustrated by **ZHU CHENG-LIANG**

WALKER BOOKS
AND SUBSIDIARIES
LONDON • BOSTON • SYDNEY • AUCKLAND

What I like most in the world is my window.

This morning, through my window,

I see the postman at the red gate.

I see a blackbird in my tree.

When I breathe on the glass

I can make drawings that quickly disappear.

My window won't change,

but the things outside will.

Some people will leave the street.
Some new people will come.
The trees will grow, and so will
the children, including me.

Here at my window
I can imagine it all.
This window is what
I like most in the world.

Except for apricot jam.

My grandmother makes it in a huge copper pot,
and her house smells of apricots for hours.
She gives everyone a jar.
When our jar is nearly empty,
I only put a tiny bit on my toast, to make the jam last.

Apricot jam is what I like most in the world.

Except for these shoes.

They have lights that flash, to show where I am going.

I can walk and run and jump in them.

My feet do a tiny bounce with every step.

One day the shoes will wear out,

or my feet will grow too big for them.

Right now they are what I like most in the world.

Except for the river.

Trees grow all along the river.
Fish and ducks live in it, and once I saw an otter.
Today the river is as shiny as a mirror.
We sit on the big rock that is like an island.

In winter the river is huge
and races along.
In summer it is shallow
and we can paddle right across it.

The river changes,
but it is always the river.
That is why I like it most
in the world.

Except for this pencil.

It is red outside and red inside.
Its colour comes out like a red ribbon.
When you sharpen it the point gets small and fine
and the pencil gets shorter.
Someday it will be all used up, and it will disappear.

It is what I like most in the world.

Except for chips.

When I smell them cooking
I get to the table before they do.
I like them best when they are almost too hot.
I dip every chip in the middle of my egg.
When the egg is finished I dip my chips in ketchup.

Soon my plate is empty.
Chips are what I like most in the world.

Except for this book.

It has a story about someone quite like me.

I know it off by heart, but I still want to hear it again.

I can say it in my head and see the pictures.

It is a funny book. It is interesting.

Maybe when I am bigger I won't want to read it every day.

But for now it is what I like most in the world.

Except for this teddy.

When I got him, he was the same size as me.

Now I am bigger than him.

He comes everywhere with me.

He sleeps with me. He is a good friend,

and I will always have him.

He is what I like most in the world.

Except for you.

You have been here since before I was born.

You look after me.

Mostly we have good times.

Even when we are cross with each other,

we belong together.

And even though you change

and I change ...

you are what I like

the very, very most in the world.

Mary Murphy, renowned for her fresh, bold artwork and warm, colourful graphics, has written and illustrated over 40 books, mainly for babies and toddlers, including *I Kissed the Baby*, *Little Owl and the Star*, *Utterly Lovely One*, *A Kiss Like This* and *Say Hello Like This*. *What I Like Most* is a rare event, where Mary's warm, lyrical writing is partnered with another illustrator. Mary lives in Dublin, Ireland, and you can find her online at marymurphy.ie.

Zhu Cheng-Liang is a Chinese illustrator with over 50 picture books to his name, including *The Sparkling Rabbit-Shaped Lamp*, which received an Honorable Mention in UNESCO's Noma Concours for Picture Book Illustrations and *A New Year's Reunion*, which won the Feng Zikai Children's Picture Book Award and a *New York Times* Best Illustrated Book Award. His most recent picture book, *Don't Let the Sun Fall*, was awarded a Biennial of Illustration Bratislava Golden Apple Award. Born in Shanghai, he now lives in Nanjing, China.